1978.
D. SPINK.

Dean's Gift Book of Hans Christian Andersen Fairy Tales

Illustrated by

Janet & Anne Grahame Johnstone

PRINTED IN GREAT BRITAIN
DEAN & SON Ltd.
52/54 Southwark St. LONDON SE1 1UA
TRADE MARK

This edition published 1975

A selection of the illustrations and stories in this gift book have been previously published in Gold Sta Book of Fairy Tales and Book of Famous Fairy Tale

603 07508 8

Little Ida's Flowers

"LOOK at my poor flowers," said pretty little Ida. "Yesterday they were so lovely and today they are all drooping. Why?"

She asked the student, who was sitting beside her.

He was a great favourite of Ida's because he told her pretty stories and made paper cut-outs of little dancing ladies, animals and tall castles.

"Your flowers went to a ball last night," said the student. "They are tired now, and that is why they hang their heads."

"But flowers can't dance!" Ida exclaimed.

"Oh, yes," replied the student, "when you are asleep in bed, all the flowers jump about merrily. They hold their dances at the Royal Summer Palace. The two most beautiful roses sit on the throne and act as King and Queen. The violets are midshipmen and the crocuses young ladies. The lilies and tulips are the dowagers and they watch to see that the young people behave with perfect propriety."

Little Ida loved this story, but the old Counsellor, who had come on a visit, thought it a great deal of rubbish.

"You should not put such nonsense into the child's head," he scolded the student.

When Ida went to bed she could not help thinking of the flowers' ball at the Palace.

She even whispered to her mother's flowers, that stood in pots on the window-sill, "I know you are going to dance tonight." But the flowers never moved.

Ida had put her own flowers into her doll's bed, so that they could rest. Sophy, the doll, looked a little cross about it.

During the night Ida awoke and heard faint music. She crept out of bed. Oh! How wonderful!

All the flowerpots were empty and the flowers were dancing. They fetched Ida's flowers from Sophy's bed and they danced most gracefully.

The dolls joined in and the flowers were so nice to Sophy that she said kindly that she did not mind giving up her bed for one night.

"Tell Ida to bury us in the morning," said the flowers, "and we will grow up even more beautiful next year."

Then they said goodnight to each other and Ida crept back to bed again.

Next morning she went to look at her flowers and found them very faded.

Sophy, the doll, looked sleepy and never gave Ida the message from the flowers.

But Ida knew just what to do.

She chose a lovely little green pasteboard box covered in flowers and birds.

"This shall be your coffin," she told the flowers. "My two Norwegian cousins are coming to stay with me, and we shall bury you in the garden."

And so they did.

The two Norwegian cousins, Jonas and Adolph, had new crossbows that their father had given them.

Ida told her cousins that her poor flowers were dead and they had a procession. The two boys marched in front, with their crossbows slung on their shoulders.

Then they buried the flowers and Jonas and Adolph fired a salute over the grave with their bows, as they had no guns or cannon.

The Steadfast Tin Soldier

THERE were once five and twenty tin soldiers, all brothers, for they had all been made out of one old tin ladle.

They carried muskets and stood stiffly at attention and their uniforms were splendid in red and blue.

The first thing in the world they heard, when the lid was taken off their box, were the words—"Tin Soldiers!"

It was a little boy, clapping his hands as he spoke.

The soldiers were his birthday present and now he set them out on the table. The soldiers were exactly alike, except one, who was slightly different from all the rest. He had but one leg. He had been made last, when there was not quite enough tin left. However, he stood as firmly as the others did on two.

It is this soldier whose adventures seem to us to be worth telling.

On the table, where the tin soldiers were set out, were other playthings, the most charming of which was a pretty pasteboard castle. Through its little windows one could look into the rooms.

In front of the castle some tiny trees stood round a small mirror, which represented a lake. Wax swans swam on the lake and were reflected in its surface.

It was all very pretty, but far the prettiest was a little damsel standing in the open doorway of the castle. Like the castle, she was made of pasteboard; but her frock was of finest muslin; a little sky-blue ribbon was flung over her shoulder like a scarf, and fastened in the middle with a bright gold spangle.

The little lady stretched out both her arms, for she was a dancer, and raised one leg so high that the Tin Soldier could not see it, and imagined that she, like him, had only one leg.

"That would be just the wife for me," thought he, "but then, she is rather too grand. She lives in a castle. I only live in a box; besides, there are twenty-five of our men in it. It's no place for her! Still, there's no harm in making her acquaintance."

So he lay down behind a snuff-box that stood on the table; from here he had a good view of the delicate little lady, who still stood on one leg, without losing her balance.

When evening came, the other Tin Soldiers were put away into the box and the people of the house went to bed.

Now it was the toys' turn to play. They pretended to visit, fight battles and give dances.

The Tin Soldiers rattled the lid of their box, they wanted to join in, but it would not open. The nut-crackers cut capers, the slate pencil did sums on the slate. There was such a noise that the canary woke up and began to sing—in verse, what is more!

The only two who did not move from their places were the Tin Soldier and the Little Dancer. She remained on tip-toe with arms outstretched; he stood steadfastly on his one leg, never moving his eyes from her face.

Twelve o'clock struck—Crack! Open sprang the lid of the snuff-box; but there was no snuff inside, only a little black conjuror—that was the fun of it!

"Tin Soldier!" cried the Conjuror. "Keep your eyes to yourself!"

But the Tin Soldier pretended not to hear.

"Well, wait till tomorrow," said the Conjuror.

When it was morning and the children were up, the Tin Soldier was put on the window-sill and whether it was the wind or the little Conjuror, I don't know, but suddenly the window flew open and the Tin Soldier fell head over heels from the third floor to the ground. What a dreadful fall! He landed on his head with his leg in the air and his bayonet wedged between the paving stones.

The Nurserymaid and the little boy came straight down to look for him, but though they nearly stood on him, they did not see him.

If the Tin Soldier had only called out "Here I am!" they must have found him. But, he did not think it correct for a man in uniform.

Now it began to rain; each drop heavier than the last, and there was a real downpour. When it was over two street boys came by.

"Look!" cried one. "Here is a Tin Soldier! He shall go for a sail."

So they made a boat out of a newspaper, put the Tin Soldier in it, and away he sailed down the gutter. Both boys ran beside him clapping their hands.

The paper boat rocked and spun, so that the Tin Soldier became quite giddy; but he remained steadfastly at attention, and held his musket tightly. All at once the boat shot under a gutter board into a long tunnel as dark as his box had been.

"Where am I going now?" he wondered. "Oh dear! This is all the Conjuror's doing! Ah! If only the Little Dancer were sailing with me. I would not care if it were twice as dark!"

Just then a great water rat, that lived in the tunnel, darted out.

"Have you a passport?" asked the Rat. "Out with your passport!"

But the Tin Soldier was silent; the boat sailed on.

"Stop him! Stop him!" screeched the Rat to the sticks and straw in the water. "He hasn't paid the toll!" And the Rat bared his sharp teeth, but the stream was strong and the Tin Soldier was whirled on in his boat.

The daylight showed ahead; then there was a mighty sound of roaring water and the boat shot out of the drain tunnel and fell with a rush into a canal.

The paper boat became damp and soft and filled with water. As the waves closed over his head the Tin Soldier thought of the pretty little Dancer he would never see again.

This song rang in his ears:

"On, through danger, Warrior brave,
Maybe to a Soldier's Grave."

Then the paper boat split asunder and the Tin Soldier fell through and was immediately swallowed by a fish.

The fish twisted and leapt and eventually became quite still. After a while there was a flash, like lightning; the daylight streamed in and a voice said:

"Oh! A Tin Soldier." It was a servant girl in a kitchen. The fish had been caught, taken to market, sold and was now being prepared as a meal.

The girl picked up the soldier and carried him upstairs for the children to see.

And how could anything be so astonishing? The Tin Soldier was back in the room he had been in before.

He saw the same children and the same toys; among the toys the same beautiful little castle and pretty dancing lady.

The Tin Soldier was so moved that he felt just like weeping tin tears, but that would have been most unsoldierly. He stood and gazed at the Little Dancer steadfastly and she looked at him.

Suddenly, for no reason, one of the little boys seized the Tin Soldier and threw him into the stove. The little Conjuror in the snuff-box must have had something to do with it.

The Soldier stood in a blaze of flame. He lost his colour and started to melt. But he bravely shouldered his musket and stood stiffly, gazing in adoration at the Little Dancer.

A door opened, a gust of air caught the Dancer and like a fairy she flew into the stove to the Tin Soldier; the blaze flared up and they were gone.

The Soldier melted into a solid lump and, when the maid cleared the stove the next day, she found him.

A little heart-shaped piece of tin and beside it a spangle, all that remained of the Dancer.

The Happy Family

THE largest leaves you can find anywhere in the country are burdock leaves.

They are so large that if a little girl takes one and holds it in front of her frock, it is big enough for an apron; and if she puts it on her head it would do for an umbrella.

Burdock leaves always grow together; they are sociable leaves and beautiful too, but all their beauty is food for the snails.

The big white snails that the grand people used to have fried. The big snails loved to gobble the burdock leaves and thought themselves very grand indeed.

"For," said the snails, "the burdock leaves were planted specially to feed us, so that we may be taken to the Manor House, cooked and laid on silver dishes."

But the two old snails were the last of their race and the Manor House had fallen down long ago. There were no silver dishes either. The burdock leaves had spread over the whole garden, even over the paths.

The two old snails were quite certain that they were the most important creatures in the whole world.

They were lonely, but very happy. They had adopted an ordinary little garden snail as their son, for they had no children of their own.

As the garden snail was a different species, he could not grow big

like the white snails, but Mother Snail insisted that he was growing all the time and Father Snail agreed. He touched the little snail's house and said that Mother Snail was right.

When the rain drummed heavily on the burdock leaves the snails went into their shell houses, and thought how lucky they were to be provided with such houses and such a great burdock wood.

"It is easy to see that we are most important people," they said.

One day Mother Snail decided that their son must have a wife.

They wondered if there were any other white snails on the other side of the wood.

They thought the Black Snails with no shells were very inferior, and when the ant suggested that their son should marry the Queen Ant, they were extremely scornful.

So they sent the Gnats who hovered all round the burdock grove to search for their son's bride.

"We know of a charming little snail," said the Gnats. "She lives very near here, in a gooseberry bush."

"Well, she must come to our son," said the big white snails. "She has only a gooseberry bush and he has a whole burdock forest."

So the little snail came and they had a very quiet wedding.

Father Snail found it very tiring, but Mother Snail made a speech.

She promised the little snails that if they lived peacefully and honestly and had lots of children, they should inherit the burdock grove. And in the end, they and their children would be taken to the Manor House, cooked and laid on silver dishes.

But the old snails never had the least idea what would happen after that.

As the Manor House had fallen down, nothing ever did happen.

And the snail family lived happily ever after, and thought that the burdock leaves and the pattering rain and the sunshine were just made for them.

Ole Luckoie: or the Dustman

OLE LUCKÖIE, the sleepy-dustman, knows the most wonderful stories in the world.

When the children are sitting quietly at the table, or on their little chairs, he comes up very softly and throws magic dust in their eyes. Then he breathes on their necks and they feel so sleepy.

But he does them no harm, it is only that they must be quiet, so that he can tell them his stories.

When they are asleep the Dustman sits on the bed. His coat is of silk and changes colour constantly,

Monday

now green, now red, now blue. Under each arm he holds an umbrella. One umbrella has pictures on it, and the Dustman holds it over good children. Then they sleep sweetly and have delightful dreams. The other umbrella has no pictures and this he holds over naughty children. They sleep heavily and wake having had no dreams at all.

Here are seven stories that the Dustman told to a little boy called Hialmar.

Ole Lucköie came every evening for a whole week to Hialmar. There are seven stories because the week has seven days.

"Listen to me," said Ole Lucköie, as soon as he had got Hialmar into his bed. "First I will decorate your room."

As he spoke the flowers in pots beside the bed grew right up and made the bedroom into a bower.

Branches grew up the walls and along the ceiling. These branches were full of sweet smelling flowers, beautiful shining fruits and lovely little dumplings full of currants.

At the same time a moaning and groaning could be heard from the drawer in the bedside table.

In there was Hialmar's slate, with the pencil to write on it and the sponge to clean it off.

The numbers in the sum written on the slate were pushing and shoving. Hialmar had put in a wrong figure and the other numbers were trying to squeeze it out. The pencil jumped about like a little dog, trying to help.

Near the slate lay Hialmar's copy book. The moaning and groaning came from the book.

Hialmar's writing was dreadfully crooked and all the letters were falling over and bumping into each other.

The copy letter at the beginning of each line taught the others.

"This is the way to stand," said the copy letter.

"Oh! But we can't!" moaned Hialmar's letters, falling about and slipping off the lines. "We're so badly made."

"Then you shall have some of the children's medicine," said the copy letter.

"Oh! No!" cried the naughty crooked letters, and they all stood up on the lines, beautifully straight.

"Now, I cannot tell you any more stories," said the Dustman. "I must drill these letters—Left, right! Left, right! Left, right!"

So he drilled the letters until they were absolutely as perfect as the copy letter.

But when Hialmar peeped into his book in the morning, the letters were as miserably bad as before.

Tuesday

AS soon as Hialmar was in bed the next night, the Dustman touched all the pieces of furniture in the room.

The pieces of furniture began to talk and they all talked about nothing but themselves.

There was a big painting in the room. It was a landscape, in it were tall trees, flowers, a wood, and a splendid castle. Also a river that flowed down to the sea.

The Dustman touched the picture with his wand and the whole thing came alive. The birds sang, the trees rustled and waved their branches and the clouds and shadows flew across the landscape.

Then the Dustman lifted little Hialmar up to the picture and the little boy put his legs inside the frame.

There he stood in the grass. He ran down to the river and sat in a little red and white boat. It had silk sails and was drawn by six swans. The swans had golden wreaths round their slender necks and blue stars on their heads.

All along the river the trees told stories about robbers and witches.

The flowers told fairy tales and talked of what the butterflies had said to them.

Gorgeous fishes with glittering gold or silver scales swam beside the boat and sometimes leapt into the air so that the water splashed over Hialmar's head.

The cockchafers opened their golden wings and said:

"Boom! Boom!"

They all wanted to go with Hialmar and each had a long story to tell.

It was a pleasant sail.

Palaces of marble or glass stood near the river and in the palaces were little princesses.

The princesses were all little girls that Hialmar knew well. He had played with them. They offered him pretty sugar toys.

Each castle had a little prince on guard outside. The princes had sabres of gold and they threw Hialmar handfuls of raisins and tin soldiers.

They were truly princes!

The Dustman told stories to the flowers and birds and beasts as well.

Wednesday

OH, how it poured with rain! Hialmar could hear it even in his sleep.

When the Dustman opened the window the water came up to the ledge and there was a large lake outside. On the lake was a magnificent ship.

"Would you like to be a voyager, Little Hialmar?" asked Ole Luckōie. "You can visit foreign lands in the night and be back next morning."

Hialmar was so excited that he could only laugh and nod his head.

Suddenly the little boy found himself in his best Sunday suit.

The weather cleared miraculously and there he was in the great ship, sailing down the streets near his house, round the church and out to the wide sea.

Hialmar was amazed. He could not quite believe this was happening to him.

Soon they could see no dry land, only a flock of great white storks.

The storks had flown from Denmark, where Hialmar lived and were going to a warm land.

They flew one behind the other and had already flown far, so far.

Little Hialmar thought he had never before seen such a wonderful sight. Then he noticed that one young stork was so weary that he could fly no farther; his wings could scarcely hold him up.

The others left him far behind and he sank lower and lower. His wings touched the ship's rigging, he slid down the sail and landed, flop, on the deck.

The ship's boy put the stork in the poultry pen where the hens, duck and turkeys were kept.

The poor stork stood among all the birds, looking quite confused.

How they clucked, quacked and gobbled.

"He is so stupid, so stupid!"

"What charming, slender legs you have!" gobbled one of the turkeys. "How much did they cost a yard?"

"Quack! Quack!" giggled the duck, but the young stork hung his head sadly.

The poultry made a shocking noise with their amusement and the young stork looked very unhappy.

Hialmar could stand the noise no longer and went to the poultry pen. He opened the door and let out the stork.

The stork was rested now, and he thanked Hialmar for helping him by bowing deeply before he flew away.

Hialmar watched as the stork flew until he was so far away that he was just a speck in the sky. Then he turned to the hens, duck and turkeys and looked quite crossly at them.

"You shall all be made into soup tomorrow," he said to the noisy poultry.

As he said it, he awoke and was surprised to find himself in his own bed. What a strange journey the Dustman had taken him that night!

Thursday

"LOOK!" said Ole Lucköie to Hialmar. "Do not be frightened, you shall see a little mouse." He held the pretty little creature out on his hand. "She has come to invite you to a wedding," the Dustman continued. "Two mice live here and they wish to set up house together. These mice live under the floor of your mother's larder; it seems a most delicious home."

"Oh, I should like to go to a mouse wedding," said Hialmar, "but how shall I get into a tiny mouse-hole?"

"Leave it to me," said the Dustman. "I will make you very tiny."

He touched Hialmar with his magic wand, and the little boy shrank until he was the size of a finger.

Hialmar felt very strange, being so small, but he knew that he could trust Ole Lucköie.

"Now," said the Dustman, "you shall borrow one of your tin soldier's uniforms. It looks so smart to wear a uniform when one is in society, especially at a wedding."

"Oh, yes," agreed Hialmar, and in a second he was dressed like the smartest little tin soldier.

The little boy marched up and down, then stood at attention, just to show Ole Lucköie what a good soldier he was.

"Would you be so kind as to sit in your mother's thimble?" asked the mouse. "It will be like a little carriage, and I will be honoured to draw you to the wedding."

"Will you really give yourself so much trouble?" said Hialmar, and in this carriage he was taken to the ceremony.

"Does not it smell nice?" said the mouse that pulled the thimble. "The passage is all decorated with bacon rind. What could be better?"

Hialmar thought the decorations very strange, but did not say so to the little mouse.

They went along a corridor under the floor. It was lighted by burning tinder torches and was just tall enough for the thimble carriage to pass through.

When they arrived at the room where the wedding was to be held, all the lady mice stood on the right, whispering and giggling together. On the left stood all the gentlemen mice, stroking their whiskers with their paws.

In the middle stood the bride and groom, kissing and cuddling each other all the time.

There was a dreadful squeezing and pushing of mice during the ceremony. The room was decorated with bacon rind, and this was all they ate. But, for pudding they had a dried pea, into which the young mice of the family had nibbled the initials of the bridal couple.

Such a charming idea!

All the mice said that the wedding had been most refined.

Hialmar then went home in his little carriage.

He had enjoyed the wedding very much and felt he had been in very distinguished company, but was not quite sure that it was not a little inferior to become so small and have to borrow a uniform from one of the tin soldiers.

Friday

"IT is amazing," said the Dustman, "how many grown-up people want me to come to them at night, especially if they've been wicked. They complain of bad dreams and offer me money. But, I do not come for money."

"Where are we going tonight, please?" asked Hialmar.

"Maybe you would care to go to another wedding," replied Ole Luckõie. "Your sister's big doll, Bertha, is to marry Herman, the large gentleman doll."

"Oh yes, I know that," said Hialmar. "When the dolls need new clothes my sister makes them have a wedding, or says it's their birthday. It's happened a hundred times."

"Ah! But tonight is their hundred and first wedding; after that there can be no more," said the Dustman. "And it will be a wonderful wedding!"

Hialmar looked at the table where the dolls' house stood. All the windows were alight inside, and outside the tin soldiers stood and presented arms.

The bride and groom sat on the floor, leaning against the table leg and looked very thoughtful. Perhaps they had cause to do so.

Now the Dustman put on his grandmother's black gown and married the dolls.

When the ceremony was over, all the furniture in the dolls' house sang this song which had been written by the lead pencil.

"We sing a song of kind farewell,
As a wedding surprise for the Beau and
  Belle.
With their kid leather skin and glassy stare,
Straight as a yardstick stand the pair.
Hurrah! Hurrah! Now sing together,
With all your breath for wood and leather!"

Then the couple were given their present. However, they could not accept anything eatable; love was enough for them to live upon.

And when the dolls had decided where to go for their honeymoon, the wedding was over.

Saturday

"NOW may I have some stories?" asked little Hialmar, as soon as the Dustman had put him to bed.

"We have to be quick this evening," said the Dustman, spreading his beautiful picture umbrella over the little boy. "Look at these Chinamen."

The umbrella was just like a big Chinese bowl with a pattern of blue trees and little pointed bridges that arched over a river.

Little Chinese men and women stood nodding their heads. Then the picture faded.

"Tomorrow," said the Dustman, "it is a feast-day; it is Sunday. Before then all the world must be put in order.

"I must go to the church tower and see that the little church goblins are polishing the bells properly to make them ring well with a beautiful sound.

"I must go to the fields and see that the wind is blowing all the dust off the grass and leaves.

"I must take down the stars in order that I may brighten them up. This is my most difficult job. First, I have to number all the stars, then I put them into my apron. The holes that the stars came from must be numbered too, so that they are all put back in their proper places.

"They must fit firmly or we shall have too many shooting stars, falling in the sky."

"Now, listen to me, Mr. Ole Luckōie," said the old portrait that hung on the wall in Hialmar's bedroom, near his bed.

"Do you know that I am little Hialmar's Great Grandfather?"

Ole Luckōie looked up at the portrait and nodded.

"It is very kind of you to tell the boy stories," continued the portrait, "but you must not muddle him by talking nonsense.

"The stars cannot be taken down and polished! They are spheres like our earth. That is absolutely correct."

"Thank you, old Great Grandfather," replied the Dustman. "Many thanks! You are indeed the Head of the Family, and very old. But, I am older still; I am an old pagan. The Greeks and Romans called me the God of Dreams. I have been into the greatest houses in the world, and I go there still. I know how to keep company with old and young, great and small.

"Now it is your turn, say what you like!"

And Ole Luckōie went away carrying his umbrella.

"You see! It is no longer possible to say what one thinks," muttered the old portrait.

And soon Hialmar woke up.

Sunday

"GOOD evening," said the Dustman and Hialmar bowed to him, then jumped quickly out of bed and turned the portrait of his Great Grandfather to face the wall.

"Now you can tell me about 'The Five Green Peas who lived in a Pod' and 'Cocky who courted Henny Penny' and 'The Darning Needle who thought she was a fine Embroidery Needle'."

"No, one can have too much of a good thing," said the Dustman. "I will show you my brother. He never comes more than once to anyone. Whomsoever he visits he takes up on his beautiful horse and tells him a story. He only knows two stories. One story is marvellously beautiful and the other is horrible beyond description."

And the Dustman lifted little Hialmar onto the window sill and said:

"There is my brother, the other Dustman. He is called Death. You see, he is not frightening at all, as he seems in picture books. Look at his beautiful silver embroidered uniform and his fine black cloak floating out behind him. See how swiftly his horse gallops."

And Hialmar saw the other Dustman ride by. He took old and young on his horse and they all had to show him their books.

Those who had "Very Good" or "Excellent" were put in front of him and heard the beautiful story. But those who had "Mediocre" or "Bad" went up behind him and had to listen to the horrible story. No matter how they shouted and tried to jump down.

"Death is a very beautiful Dustman," said Hialmar. "I am not afraid of him."

"No, you must not be frightened of him," said Ole Lucköie, "but you must be careful to have a good report to show him."

"This is very instructional," said the portrait of the old Great Grandfather. "I approve. It all comes from giving my opinion."

He was contented.

These are the stories of the Dustman. Perhaps he will come and tell you a story tonight.

The Little
Match Girl

IT was frightfully cold and snow was falling, darkness was closing in; it was New Year's Eve, the last day of the year.

In the cold and darkness wandered a little girl, bareheaded and with bare feet, too. True, she had slippers on when she started from home, but they had not been much use. They had been much too large for her, great big slippers; her mother had used them last. The little girl had lost them as she scuttled across the street to avoid two carriages that had been rushing down the road towards her.

One slipper had quite disappeared, and a naughty boy had run off with the other, shouting that he would use it as a cradle when he had children of his own.

Now the little girl walked on barefooted, and her feet were red and blue with cold; she wore a tattered old apron in which she carried bundles of sulphur matches to sell, and she held another bunch in her hand. She had not sold any matches that day; in fact no one had given her so much as a halfpenny. Poor little thing, she looked so sad as she trudged shivering through the town, cold and hungry. The flakes of snow fell on her long fair hair, which curled so prettily on her neck; but she never gave a thought to her own beauty. Lights shone in the windows, and out of the houses came the delicious smell of roast goose. It was New Year's Eve, and that was what occupied her thoughts.

In the angle where two houses joined she crouched down and tucked her legs under her, but she could not get warm; she grew colder and colder. She dared not go home, for she had earned no money. Besides, her home was so cold, too; their room was right under the roof, with straw and old rags stuffed into the cracks in the walls and the tiles, and still the wind whistled through.

Her poor little hands were *so* numb; if only she dared strike a match to warm them. She took one and struck it against the brick wall. Scritch! How it spurted and flared! Oh, what a warm glow, like a little taper. She held her hands round it. How strange! To the little girl it

seemed that she was sitting in front of a beautiful big iron stove. A stove with brass fittings, shiny knob and rail, and such a wonderful warm fire. She stretched her legs out to warm them, too, and out went the flame—the stove vanished, and there she sat in the snow with the black, burnt match stub in her hand.

She struck another match. Its flame blazed, lighting the brick wall before her, which became as a gauze veil. Through it she could see a wonderful big table, laid with a snow-white cloth and lovely porcelain, glass and silver; in the centre of the table, on a dish, was a fine roast goose stuffed with apples and prunes. And, how splendid! The goose jumped off the table onto the floor and waddled towards her . . . but then out went the match, and before her was the old brick wall.

How disappointed she felt.

She kindled a third match.

Again a flame shot up—and now she was sitting under a most beautiful Christmas tree. It was even bigger, prettier and more gaily decorated than the one she had seen through the glass doors of the rich merchant's house at Christmas.

Hundreds of fine wax tapers burned on its green branches, and it was hung with pretty paper figures

who looked down at her. They were like the ones that hang in shop windows.

The match fizzled out, and the Christmas tree candles grew taller and brighter and became the stars twinkling in the night sky; one of the stars rushed down towards earth—a shooting star with a sparkling, fiery tail.

"That is someone dying," murmured the little girl. She had been told this by her grandmother. Her grandmother was dead and was the only person who had ever loved the child and been kind to her.

Suddenly her grandmother appeared before her.

"Grandmamma!" cried the child. "Oh, take me with you! Don't leave me when the match burns out, like the warm stove, the beautiful goose and the pretty Christmas tree!"

Hurriedly she lit all the matches in the bundle she held, to stop her grandmother from disappearing. And the matches burned so brilliantly that night seemed like day.

Her grandmother looked taller and more beautiful than she had ever looked in life. And she lifted the poor little girl up in her arms, and together they flew up to where there was no cold nor hunger nor fear; up to God.

In the chill early morning the little girl was found. She was sitting in between two houses, her cheeks glowed rosily and there was a smile on her lips—frozen to death on the last night of the Old Year. The matches were in her lap, one bundle quite burned up.

"She was trying to warm herself," the people said. And none knew what lovely visions she had seen, or how gloriously she and her grandmother had passed into a really new Year.

Thumbelina

ONCE upon a time there was a young woman who longed for a tiny child, but she wished in vain. So she went to an old witch woman and told her: "I have the greatest longing to have a little child of my own. Please help me."

"Ah, if you want your dream to come true," said the sorceress, "take this grain of barley. It's not the kind the peasant sows in his field or the sort you feed to the chickens. Sow it in a flowerpot, tend it and just see what happens!"

"Oh, many, many thanks!" cried the young woman, and she gave the old witch a silver shilling.

When she got home the woman planted the barley corn and immediately a big beautiful flower grew up. It was like a tulip and its red and yellow petals were tightly closed.

"It is a lovely flower," exclaimed the woman, and she kissed its petals gently. As she did this, there was a loud crack and the bud burst open. Right in the centre of the flower, on a little green pyramid, sat the tiniest, prettiest little girl. She was no bigger than your thumb, and for that reason she was called Thumbelina.

Thumbelina was given a varnished walnut shell to sleep in, with a mattress of violet petals and a charming rose-petal quilt.

One night, as the little girl lay sleeping, an ugly old toad came in and took up Thumbelina in the walnut shell and carried it off to the stream that flowed through the garden.

The old toad lived here in the mud with her son. Oh! how ugly and stupid he was!

"Koax! Koax! Beekek-ek-kex!" he croaked, staring at the pretty little damsel as she slept. He was too silly to say more.

"Hush! You will wake her!" said his mother, the toad. "She is to be your wife, so let us get the staterooms in the mud ready for your wedding."

The old toad put Thumbelina in her little bed on a huge green waterlily leaf.

"Now she cannot run away from us," she croaked.

Poor little Thumbelina woke early in the morning and wept bitterly to find herself all alone in such a strange place. Thumbelina hated the thought of marrying the young toad.

Some little fishes took pity on her and nibbled through the stem of the waterlily leaf. They thought her far too pretty to marry the foolish toad.

Thumbelina sailed down the stream and a butterfly helped her by pulling her leaf boat, harnessed with her blue sash.

All summer Thumbelina lived in the countryside and was happy but in the winter she was hungry and cold. At last she was given shelter by a kind old fieldmouse, who fed her with corn and let her stay in the snug mousehole house under the cornfield.

But the mouse wished her to marry a dull blind old mole who lived next door and was very rich. "He has a beautiful black velvet suit and a very large house," squeaked the mouse.

One evening the mole took them along a passage in his house. There lay a beautiful swallow. It seemed to be dead. Thumbelina was *so* sorry for the pretty bird. Later she slipped away and came to the swallow. She warmed it and covered it with her own quilt. Suddenly she felt its heart beating under its soft downy feathers. All winter she nursed the beautiful swallow. How sad she was when it flew away. She was to marry the mole soon and the thought made her very unhappy.

On the day of her wedding Thumbelina went sadly out into the field to say goodbye to the sun, for as the mole's wife she would live underground.

"Farewell, Sun. Farewell," she cried in despair. "Greet the dear swallow if you see him."

"Quiwit! Quiwit!" There was a fluttering of wings and there was the swallow swooping round her. The swallow easily persuaded Thumbelina to leave the cold and fly with him to the warm sunny countries. Thumbelina lay among the soft feathers on the swallow's back.

Away they flew—over forests, lakes and mountains.

At last they reached the warm lands. The

skies were blue and lemons and melons grew in groves. Children chased large butterflies.

The swallow flew on to a blue lake. There stood a half-ruined palace of white marble. The walls were covered with a flowery creeper full of swallow's nests.

On the ground among the fallen columns twined some large white flowers. Sitting in the most magnificent flower was a handsome little manikin. He wore a brilliant gold crown and on his shoulders he had bright delicate wings.

The little prince was delighted when he saw Thumbelina. He thought her quite the loveliest maiden he had ever seen. He took his golden crown and placed it on her head. He begged her to be his queen and rule with him over the flower-spirits.

Then all the flower-spirit fairies came with gifts. The finest present was a little pair of wings. The swallow sang Thumbelina his most beautiful song.

Then he flew back to Denmark where he had a little nest by the window of a man who writes stories for children.

"Quiwit! Quiwit! Quiwit!" he sang to the writer, and from him we learned the whole story.

The Top & the Ball

A TOP and Ball once lay side by side in a drawer full of toys. Said the Top to the Ball: "Why should we not become Bride and Bridegroom, seeing that we are so much thrown together?"

But the Ball would not hear of such a thing. She was made of real Moroccan leather and thought herself a very fine young lady.

Next day the little boy who owned the toys came to the drawer. He took out the Top and painted it red and yellow and drove a fine brass nail through the middle of it.

Now it was glorious to see the Top spin round.

"Look at me!" he cried to the Ball. "Now what do you say? Do let us be married. We suit each other so finely. You can jump and I can spin; we should be so very happy together."

"Do you think so?" said the Ball. "Perhaps you are not aware that my father and mother wore a pair of Moroccan slippers and I have cork in my body."

"Yes, maybe, but I am made of real mahogany," replied the Top. "The burgomaster made me with his own hands. He has his own lathe and very much enjoyed turning me."

"Can I believe this?" asked the haughty Ball.

"May I never be whipped again if I lie!" said the Top.

"You talk rather well," replied the Ball, "but I am not free. I am affianced to a young swallow. Whenever I fly up in the air he looks out of his nest and asks me to marry him. I have said 'I will' to him in my heart, which is nearly as good as a betrothal."

"That's a lot of use," grumbled the Top, and no more was said on the subject.

Next day the Ball was taken out. The Top saw her fly like a bird up into the air—so high that she disappeared. Then back she came. But every time she touched the ground she sprang higher than before. It must have been love or the cork in her body that was the reason for this.

The ninth time the Ball bounced she did not come back. The little boy looked and looked, but she had quite gone.

"I know where she is," sighed the Top. "She is in the swallow's nest celebrating her wedding."

The more he thought about the Ball, the more he loved her. Even though he knew he could not marry her, he could not stop caring about her, and he couldn't forget that Another had been preferred to himself. The Top spun and hummed just as he had always done, but always he thought about his lost love and she seemed more beautiful to him with every passing minute.

Several years passed. The Top was not young any more, but he was still very much in love with the Ball. One day he was taken and gilded all over. Now he was more handsome than ever before. He was a beautiful golden Top and he spun more quickly and hummed more loudly. Yes, he was altogether a very grand Top, he decided.

Then one day, as the little boy was playing with him out in the garden, the Top sprang too high and vanished. The little boy was very sad that he had gone and looked high and low for him. But the Top was nowhere to be found. Where could he be?

He landed in an old rain-barrel full of rubbish. Dead flowers, leaves, sweepings, and stones lay there, along with all sorts of odd things that had been washed down from the guttering.

"Alas, I shall lie amongst all this rubbish and all my gilding will be spoilt. What trumpery I am surrounded by!" said the Top.

He looked round. A horrid clump of rotten leaves lay next to him and also a peculiar round thing. Was it an old apple? No, it was not an apple—only an old Ball which had lain in the gutter for some years and was quite soggy.

"Thank goodness!" said the Ball, gazing with delight at the handsome gold Top. "Someone who is my equal for me to talk to—after all these years!" The Ball did not realise who the Top was.

"I am made of real Moroccan leather, you know," she went on. "I was sown together by a young lady's hand and I have cork in my body, too! I was betrothed to marry a handsome young swallow when I fell by accident into this horrid barrel. I have lain here for five long terrible years. I am quite soaked. My dear, it has been such a tedious thing for an elegant young lady like myself to put up with."

The Top said not a word. He thought of his long-lost love and he realised that it was she who lay in the barrel.

Then one of the maids came along. She had been told to clear out all the rubbish in the barrel and throw it away.

"Hurrah!" she cried. "Here is the gilt Top! The young Master will be pleased to have it back again!" She didn't notice the old Ball lying close beside it.

The Top was taken back to the play-room, and it was played with and admired just as much as before. But nothing more was ever heard of the Ball.

The Top sighed for her no more. He could not love her now and he felt very silly, thinking and dreaming about her for all that time when she had been lying with all that rubbish in the barrel.

"How lucky it was that *I* was rescued," he hummed as he spun.

The Darning Needle

ONCE upon a time there was a Darning Needle who thought herself very fine. She decided she wasn't really a Darning Needle at all; she was certain she was an Embroidery Needle.

"Take great care of me. Hold me tightly!" said the Darning Needle to the Fingers as they picked her up. "Don't drop me, now. I am very fine, you know. If I were to fall on the floor, you would never find me again."

"Don't worry," said the Fingers, as they held the Darning Needle round her waist.

"See. I am coming with my train," said the Darning Needle, and she drew a long thread without a single knot after her.

The Fingers took the Needle to the Cook's slipper. The leather of the uppers was torn and needed stitching together.

"Oh, this is vulgar work," complained the Darning Needle. "I shall never get through. I am too dainty. I shall break. I *am* breaking!" And break she did. "I told you so, didn't I!" she went on. "I am too fine."

"Now she is useless," thought the Fingers, but they still had to hold on. The Cook dropped sealing-wax on the Darning Needle and stuck it in her neckerchief.

"Look! Now I am a Breast-pin," said the Darning Needle, very pleased. "I knew that I was sure to become great. When one is special, one always becomes something extremely grand." And she laughed to herself,

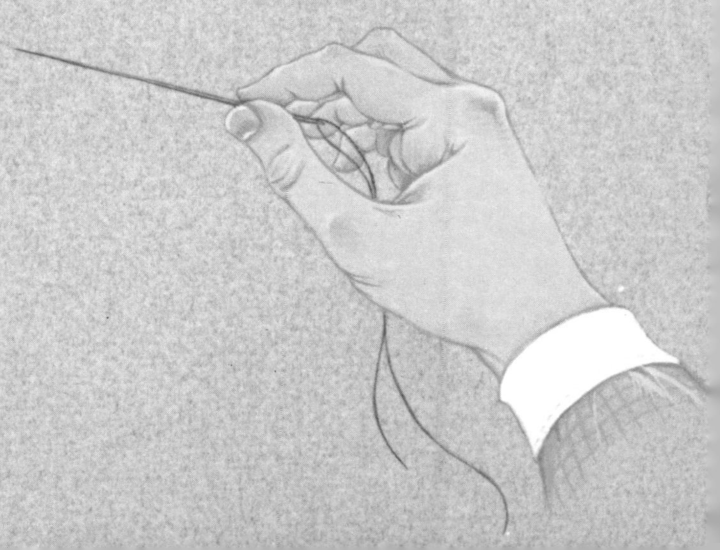

not out loud, for whoever heard a Darning Needle laugh! There she sat as proudly as a lady in a carriage.

"May I enquire if you are made of gold?" she asked the pin who was her neighbour. "You are rather pretty, but your head is peculiar. It is only small. You must see that it grows. But then, not everyone can have sealing-wax dropped on them."

Then the Darning Needle drew herself up so proudly that she fell out of the neckerchief into the sink. The cook was doing the washing-up.

"Now I am off on my travels," cried the Darning Needle excitedly. "But I do hope I shall not go too far."

However the Darning Needle did travel a long long way.

"I am too fine for this world!" said she, as she lay in the gutter. "But I shall never forget who I am." And she held herself very upright and smiled grandly.

Splinters of wood, straw, pieces of soggy newspaper and all sorts of things swirled past her.

"See how they float along!" said the Darning Needle. "They don't realise that someone as fine as myself is stuck down here. That splinter thinks of nothing but himself—pah! A mere chip! There goes a straw, twirling round and round. Don't think so much of yourself. You may bump into a stone. And that old newspaper! All that is printed upon it was forgotten years ago. Yet see how it unfolds itself. I shall sit patiently and quietly. I know my worth, and that is enough for me."

One day the Darning Needle saw something glittering brightly beside her. She was certain it was a diamond. Actually, it was a chip of bottle glass.

"How do you do. I am a Breast-pin. Surely you are a diamond?"

"Oh yes, something like that," agreed the Glass. So they each thought themselves very rare and precious, and complained of the extraordinary haughtiness of the rest of the world.

"I have come from a Lady's work-box," declared the Darning Needle. "The Lady was a cook. She had five fingers on each hand. I have never met anything as conceited as those five fingers, and yet they were only there to take me in and out of the work-box."

"Were they of noble birth? Did they shine?" asked the Bottle-glass.

"Certainly not!" replied the Darning Needle. "But how arrogant they were! 'Finger' was their surname. They stood very upright, side by side, although they were of different sizes. The first, Thumbkin, was short and fat. He sometimes stood opposite the others, and only had one bend in his back. He told me that if a person lost him, that man was no longer fit for military service. Foreman, the second one, poked into everything, dipped into sweet and sour, pointed at the sun and moon, and pressed on the pen when the Fingers wrote. Longman, the third, was a head taller than the others. Ringman, the fourth, wore a gold belt round his middle. And as for Littleman, he never did anything, and this made him proudest of all. They were so stuck-up and tiresome that I removed myself to this gutter."

"And now we sit here together and sparkle," said the Glass. Just then a deluge of water sent the splinter of Glass floating away.

"There he goes," mused the Darning Needle. "I shall remain here. I am so fine and proud of my respectability." She sat very upright, thinking lofty thoughts.

"I almost think I am the child of a sunbeam; I am so fine. But the sun cannot reach me here. Alack, even my mother cannot find me here. If I still had my eye, I might weep. But no! It is not refined to weep."

Then one day some little street urchins were wading in the gutter, poking about and hunting for pennies, odd nails and suchlike. It was very dirty work, but that made it all the more enjoyable as far as they were concerned.

"Oh! Oh!" cried one of them, pricking himself on the Darning Needle. "He is a fine fellow, though."

"I am no fellow. I am a young lady," scolded the Darning Needle, but no one heard.

She had lost her sealing-wax and had become quite black. But as black makes a person look slim, she imagined herself finer than ever.

"There sails an eggshell!" said the boys, and they stuck the Darning Needle into it.

"White walls and a lady in black. What a striking contrast!" said the Darning Needle. "Now everyone can see me! I only hope I shall not be seasick. That would be the end of everything."

But the Darning Needle was not seasick and that was not the end of her.

"Ah, I am steeled against seasickness. Here one has the advantage over man. Now the worst is over. The finer one is, the more one can bear."

"CRACK!" went the eggshell, as a wagon rolled over it.

"Ugh! What a weight!" cried the Darning Needle. "I think I shall be seasick after all. I shall break! I shall break!"But she did not break—although the wagon wheel went right over her. Long did she lie there—and there let her lie.

DEEP in the country lay the manor-house of an old squire. His oldest sons thought themselves so clever that if they had only known half of what they did know, it would have been quite enough. They both wanted to marry the King's daughter, for she had proclaimed that she would wed the man who best knew how to choose his words.

Blockhead Hans

Both prepared their wooing for a whole week, which was as long as they were allowed. But this was plenty of time, for they were both tremendously knowledgeable, and everyone knows how useful that can be. One knew the whole Latin dictionary and three years' issues of the local daily paper off by heart—recited either backwards or forwards. The other had worked at law and knew what each member of the corporation ought to do. So he considered that he could speak excellently on state matters and give his opinion. Besides this he could embroider braces with exquisite roses, posies and scrolls, for he was very quick with his fingers.

"I shall win the Princess!" they both cried.

Their old father gave each of them a fine horse. The son who knew the dictionary and the newspapers by heart had a coal-black horse, and the son who was so clever at corporation law had a milk-white one. Then they oiled the corners of their mouths to make their conversation flow. All the servants stood out in the courtyard and watched them mount their steeds.

Here too came the youngest brother for the old squire had three sons. He was not counted with the others for he was the dunce of the family and everyone called him 'Blockhead Hans'.

"Hey!" said Blockhead Hans. "Where are you going? You have your Sunday suits on!"

"We are off to Court to woo the Princess. Don't you know what the whole country knows!" And they explained that the Princess was looking for a husband and that they were going to woo her.

"Hurray! I'll go too," cried Blockhead Hans. "I must have a horse as well. How I long to be married! If she wants to have me, she *will*

"Stop all that nonsense, Hans!" said the old squire. "I am not going to give *you* a horse. You cannot speak properly; you do not know how to choose your words. Your brothers are very different lads!"

"Well," said Blockhead Hans, "if I can't have a horse, I shall ride on the goat. He is mine."

So after his brothers he went. He sat astride the goat, stuck his heels in its sides and came rattling down the road like a whirlwind.

"Hoppetty-hop! What a ride! Here I come—whoopee!" yelled Blockhead Hans, and he sang at the top of his voice so that the echoes rang both far and near.

His two brothers were ambling on in silence. They were thinking up clever remarks to say to the Princess, and when they thought of one they said it under their breath over and over again so that they knew it by heart.

"Hey!" bellowed Blockhead Hans. "Here I am! Just you look at what I have picked up on the road. You both missed it!" And he held up a dead crow. The two brothers stared at it.

"Blockhead!" they said. "Whatever are you going to do with a dead crow?"

"Why, I shall give it to the Princess!" said Blockhead Hans.

The brothers looked at each other and laughed.

"You do that!" they said. "The Princess will be delighted with a dead crow!" And they galloped on, still laughing at Hans. But he took no notice of them.

Not long afterwards the brothers heard Hans calling them again.

"Slap! Bang! Here I am again! Look what I've found now! Not something you're lucky enough to find in the road every day!"

The brothers turned round to see what it was.

"Blockhead!" they jeered. "That is an old broken wooden shoe! Is that for the Princess too?"

"Of course!" said Blockhead Hans, and his brothers tittered and rode on ahead some distance.

"Slap! Bang! Here I come again!" shouted Blockhead soon afterwards. "This is better than before. This is really splendid!"

"Now what!" said the brothers, reining in their horses.

"The Princess will marry me straight away when she sees this," said Blockhead

Hans, and he held up a large lump of mud.

"Why, this is nothing but mud—straight from the ditch," exclaimed his brothers.

"Of course!" said Blockhead Hans. "The very finest! See how it trickles through my fingers."

Blockhead Hans filled his pocket with mud from the ditch and his two brothers galloped off in a cloud of dust. Their horses' hooves struck sparks from the cobble stones. Indeed they rode so fast that they reached the King's palace a whole hour before Blockhead Hans.

As each suitor arrived, he was given a number and told to line up with the others. The suitors were queuing in rows of six, and they were so tightly packed together, they could not even raise their arms. And what a blessing this was! They would have torn each other to pieces

otherwise. They were all so jealous of one another!

Huge crowds of onlookers thronged the palace and all waited eagerly for the Princess to receive her suitors.

As each suitor came into the throne room, he was quite overcome by the richness and splendour of it all, and all his fine speeches would go clean out of his head.

"It does not matter," the Princess would say. "Away with him!"

At last she came to the row where the brother who knew the dictionary by heart was waiting his turn. But he had become more and more nervous waiting in the long queue, and now he couldn't even remember the words beginning with A! He shifted uneasily from one foot to the other and this made the floor creak. He looked up at the ceiling, and this made him feel even more confused, because the ceiling was made of mirrors, and he looked as if he was standing on his head! There was dead silence while everyone waited for him to speak. By each of four big bay windows stood a newspaper man—three reporters and an editor. They were each writing down all that was said to publish it in the penny press the very next day. But the brother was dumb, and the Princess was looking rather fidgety and impatient. The fire at one end of the room burned brightly.

"Hot, isn't it?" mumbled the tongue-tied brother at last.

"Naturally," said the Princess. "My father is roasting young chickens."

"Ahem!" said the brother and stood looking silly. He had not been

expecting such an ordinary remark from someone as extra-ordinary as a Princess, and though he longed to give a witty reply, he was quite lost for words.

"It doesn't matter," said the Princess. "Take him out!"

Then in came the other brother.

"How hot it is," he said.

"Of course! We are roasting young chickens today," said the Princess, and waited for him to say something else.

"How do you . . . er," said the brother and faltered, and each of the four newspapermen wrote down, 'How do you . . . er.'

"Never mind," said the Princess. "Away with him!"

There were hardly any suitors left now, and still the Princess hadn't found a husband. Then —clitter! Clatter! Into the splendid throne room rode Blockhead Hans on his goat. The watching courtiers gasped and stared, and the newspapermen nudged each other and sniggered.

"The Princess won't even bother to talk to him," they said.

But the Princess smiled at Blockhead Hans, and he jumped off his goat.

"Phew! How roasting hot it is in here," he said.

"Of course! We are roasting young chickens today," said the Princess.

"Fine!" said Blockhead Hans, looking very pleased. "Then can my crow roast with them?"

"With great pleasure," said the Princess, and she smiled at Hans again. "But what will you roast your crow in? For I have neither pot nor pan."

"See!" said Blockhead Hans, as he took out the old wooden shoe and tucked the dead crow into it. "Here is a cooking pot with tin rings."

"What a fine dish it will be," cried the Princess. "But we have no gravy."

"Yes, we have," said Blockhead Hans. "I've plenty in my pocket—so much that I can easily throw some away." And he tipped some of the mud in his pocket out on to the floor.

"I like you," said the Princess. "You can answer and you can speak. Yes, I shall marry you. But did you know that everything we are

saying has been taken down for tomorrow's newspapers? By each window stand three reporters and an editor, and that old editor is the worst. He doesn't understand anything!"

She said this to tease Hans. The reporters sniggered and each dropped an ink blot.

"Oh ho! Are these the great people?" said Blockhead Hans. "Then the editor shall have the best!" Saying this, he emptied his pocket and threw the mud in the editor's face.

"How neatly done!" exclaimed the Princess. "I couldn't do that, but I shall soon learn."

Blockhead Hans became King, got a wife, a crown and a throne; and this we have still damp from the presses of the editor and the reporters—and they are not to be believed for a moment.